THE HARDY BOYS CASE FILES

Undercover Brothers   Based on the series by Franklin W. Dixon

Crawling with
ZOMBIES

PAPERCUTZ

THE HARDY BOYS

THE NEW CASE FILES

Undercover Brothers

Crawling with ZOMBIES

GERRY CONWAY
Writer

PAULO HENRIQUE
Artist

Based on the series by FRANKLIN W. DIXON

PAPERCUTZ™
New York

"Crawling With Zombies"
GERRY CONWAY - Writer
PAULO HENRIQUE - Artist
LAURIE E. SMITH - Colorist
MARK LERER - Letterer
JUNTO CREATIVE - Production

MICHAEL PETRANEK
Associate Editor
JIM SALICRUP
Editor-in-Chief

ISBN: 978-1-59707-219-9 paperback edition
ISBN: 978-1-59707-220-5 hardcover edition

Printed in China
August 2010 by Regent Publishing
6/f, Hang Tung Resource Centre
No. 18 A Kung Ngam Village Road
Shau Kei Wan, Hong Kong

Distributed by Macmillan.
First Printing

YAAAYY!!

WAY TO GO, HARDY BOYS!

IT'S A *PHOTO FINISH!*

GUESS WHAT, LITTLE BROTHER?

I THINK WE *WON.*

COULD YOU DO ME A FAVOR, FRANK?

DON'T CALL ME "LITTLE BROTHER."

JOE, HEY, I DIDN'T MEAN--

YEAH, I KNOW YOU DIDN'T MEAN ANY-THING BY IT.

IT'S JUST, SOMETIMES...I GET *TIRED* OF BEING THE "YOUNGER HARDY BOY BROTHER."

WHAT'S GOING ON? WE GOT A REPORT OF *GUNSHOTS...*

THOSE GUYS PULLED GUNS ON US, OFFICERS.

I GUESS SOME PEOPLE ARE SORE LOSERS.

HUH. YOU'RE FENTON HARDY'S BOYS, AREN'T YOU?

THAT'S RIGHT, OFFICER.

YOUR OLD MAN'S A *DETECTIVE*.

THIS ISN'T PART OF SOME CRAZY AMATEUR *INVESTIGATION*, NOW, IS IT?

"*AMATEUR* INVESTIGATION," OFFICER? GOSH, NO.

WE WOULDN'T *DREAM* OF INTERFERING UNOFFICIALLY IN POLICE BUSINESS.

GOOD.

LEAVE THE POLICEWORK TO THE *PROS*, YOU TWO.

LAST THING WE NEED IS A COUPLE'A *TEENS* PLAYING CRIME-FIGHTER.

WE HEAR YOU, OFFICER.

"AMERICAN TEENS AGAINST CRIME."

THE IDEA'S *RIDICULOUS.*

FRANK, JOE... WE'VE BUMPED HEADS FROM TIME TO TIME...AND AS YOUR AUNT, I TAKE *RESPONSIBILITY* FOR THAT.

SOMETIMES I FORGET WHAT IT'S LIKE TO BE A *TEENAGER*...

...EVEN THOUGH IT WASN'T THAT *LONG AGO* I WAS A TEEN MYSELF.

SO, TO MAKE AMENDS FOR ANY BAD FEELINGS BETWEEN US, AND IN HONOR OF THE *ANNIVERSARY* OF MY COMING TO STAY WITH YOU AND YOUR PARENTS...

AUNT TRUDY, HONESTLY, YOU DIDN'T HAVE TO.

...I GOT YOU *THIS*.

BUT HEY, AS LONG AS YOU DID, *THANKS*.

SO WHAT *IS* IT?

WELL, I KNOW HOW YOU BOYS LOVE YOUR *VIDEO GAMES*.

AND SINCE THE MAN AT THE ELECTRONICS SHOP IN THE MALL SAID *GAME CARTRIDGE CONSOLES* ARE "SO 1999--"

I DONATED YOUR *OLD* GAME CONSOLE TO A CHILDREN'S CHARITY AND BOUGHT YOU THIS BRAND NEW *ZBOX SYSTEM*.

IT PLAYS *DVDs* AND *STREAMS VIDEO* FROM THE INTERNET, *AND* IT SYNCS WITH YOUR *CELLPHONE* AND MP3 PLAYER.

THE MAN AT THE MALL SAYS IT'S A *COMPLETE HOME ENTERTAINMENT SYSTEM*.

AUNT TRUDY, YOU GAVE OUR *OLD* GAME CONSOLE TO *CHARITY?*

WITHOUT *ASKING* US?

THE MAN AT THE MALL SAID IT WAS *OUT OF DATE.*

HONESTLY, I THOUGHT YOU'D BE *GRATEFUL.*

I TRY TO BE NICE, AND THIS IS THE *THANKS* I GET?

FRANK AND JOE HARDY, YOU SHOULD BE *ASHAMED.*

B-BUT, MOM--

SHE DIDN'T--WE DIDN'T--

ZBOX

YOUR MOTHER'S RIGHT, BOYS. YOU OWE AUNT TRUDY A BIG *THANK YOU.*

WHY, WHEN SHE TOLD ME WHAT SHE WAS DOING, I EVEN GOT YOU A *NEW GAME* FOR YOUR *NEW CONSOLE.*

OH. A *NEW* GAME. FOR OUR *NEW* GAME CONSOLE. THAT'S, UH, *TERRIFIC.*

AUNT TRUDY, WE ARE *SO, SO, SO* SORRY FOR NOT BEING MORE GRATEFUL.

YOU ARE THE BEST AUNT *EVER.* SERIOUSLY.

THANKYOU THANKYOU THANKYOU

"... UNTIL ONE OF THE 'ZOMBIE' PARTICIPANTS STEPPED *OFF* A SIDEWALK AND INTO THE *PATH* OF AN ONCOMING CAR."

LUCKILY, THE GIRL *SURVIVED.*

SHE TOLD INVESTIGATORS SHE HAD NO IDEA WHAT *COMPELLED* HER TO STEP IN FRONT OF THAT CAR.

SINCE THEN, THERE HAVE BEEN HALF A DOZEN *SIMILAR* INCIDENTS IN AND AROUND BAYPORT.

EACH TIME, AFFECTED "ZOMBIES" REPORTED LOSING *COMPLETE CONTROL* OF THEIR OWN ACTIONS...

"... AS IF SOME *OUTSIDE FORCE* HAD TAKEN OVER THEIR MINDS.

"WHAT BEGAN AS A HARMLESS PRANK HAS BECOME A *DEADLY DANGER* TO ALL THOSE INVOLVED."

BECAUSE *ZOMBIE CRAWLS* ARE ORGANIZED *ANONYMOUSLY*--VIA *SMS* TEXTS, ONLINE SOCIAL NET-WORK UPDATES, TWITTER ALERTS--

AUTHORITIES HAVE BEEN *UNABLE* TO DISCOVER *WHO'S* BEHIND THIS, AND *WHY.*

THAT'S WHERE YOU COME IN, HARDY BOYS.

FIND OUT WHAT'S REALLY GOING ON, *BEFORE* SOMEONE AT ONE OF THESE CRAWLS GETS *KILLED.*

WOW.

SOCIAL NETWORKING... ISN'T THAT SOMETHING YOUR GIRLFRIEND *BELINDA CONRAD* IS INTO?

SHE'S NOT MY "GIRLFRIEND," JOE. I DON'T HAVE TIME FOR THAT SORT OF THING, AND EVEN IF I DID--

EVEN IF YOU DID, YOU'D BE TOO TONGUE-TIED TO KNOW HOW TO GET *STARTED* WITH A GIRL IN THE FIRST PLACE.

BUT THE POINT IS, BELINDA MIGHT KNOW HOW TO FIND OUT WHEN AND WHERE THE NEXT ONE OF THESE *ZOMBIE CRAWLS* IS SCHEDULED TO GO DOWN.

CHET TOLD ME LAST NIGHT SHE WAS GOING OVER TO HIS HOUSE THIS AFTERNOON TO CRAM FOR A HISTORY TEST.

MAYBE WE SHOULD THINK THIS THROUGH--

AW, C'MON, "BIG BROTHER."

JUST THIS ONCE, LET'S *GO* FIRST, AND *THINK* LATER!

CHAPTER THREE: TWO'S COMPANY, THREE'S A CROWD

UH, BELINDA, COULD YOU --

OUTTA MY WAY, CHET.

Y'KNOW, BELINDA, IF IT WAS *ME* ASKING *YOU* FOR HELP LIKE THIS, I'D WANT TO PAY YOU BACK BY TAKING YOU OUT TO DINNER SOMEPLACE NICE.

SOMEPLACE *EXPENSIVE.*

NOT TO MENTION MAYBE *ROMANTIC.*

YOU DO REALIZE I'M GOING TO KILL YOU FOR THIS, RIGHT, JOE?

OWW.

IN CASE ANYBODY CARES, THAT ELBOW-JAB KINDA *HURT.*

GOT IT.

ACCORDING TO A POST ON THE #ZOMBIECRAWL HASHTAG ON THE TWEESTER FEED, THERE'S A "ZOMBIE CRAWL" SCHEDULED TONIGHT FOR MUSEUM ROW IN BAYPORT.

AND, FRANK, JUST SO YOU KNOW, I LOVE ITALIAN FOOD, BUT IN A PINCH, I COULD ALSO GO FOR SOME REALLY GOOD CHINESE.

UH... ITALIAN.

I'LL, UH, YEP, *RIGHT*...ITALIAN. DINNER.

SOUNDS GREAT. CAN'T WAIT.

ME NEITHER. NOW THAT WE KNOW WHERE THE ZOMBIES ARE *CRAWLIN'*, LET'S GET *HOPPIN'* BEFORE THEY START *DROPPIN'*.

WHOA, WAIT, *SLOW DOWN*, LITTLE BROTHER.

BEFORE WE DO ANYTHING WE'VE GOT TO MAKE A *PLAN*.

SO WHAT DO WE DO *NOW?*

MAYBE HAVE THAT ITALIAN DINNER WE WERE TALKING ABOUT?

HINT, HINT?

NO, WHAT WE *DO* IS FIGURE OUT WHO *SENT* THE #ZOMBIE-CRAWL HASH-TAG MESSAGE ORGANIZING TONIGHT'S ZOMBIE CRAWL.

WHOEVER SENT THAT MESSAGE MUST KNOW WHAT'S *BEHIND* ALL THIS.

RATS.

FIRST TIME IN A WHILE I GET YOU ALONE AND YOU STILL WANT TO PLAY *DETECTIVE.*

I DON'T "PLAY" DETECTIVE.

I AM A DETECTIVE.

>SIGH!<

OH.

ACROSS TOWN, AT BAYPORT HIGH...

...BUT THE ONE WE WANT IS THE ACCOUNT THAT WAS *ONLINE* WHEN THAT TWEESTER UPDATE WAS SENT.

"TAYLOR DENT."
IT SAYS HERE SHE'S IN OUR GRADE, BUT I DON'T *KNOW* HER, AND I USED TO THINK I KNEW *EVERYBODY*...

LOOKS LIKE THERE'RE SEVERAL *USER ACCOUNTS* ON THIS COMPUTER...

THAT'S NO BIG SURPRISE. *NOBODY* KNOWS ME HERE.

YOU'RE TAYLOR?

DID YOU SEND OUT A TWEESTER MESSAGE ANNOUNCING A *ZOMBIE CRAWL* FOR TONIGHT?

M—MAYBE.

WHILE, FOR STARTERS, IF *YOU* CALLED FOR A CRAWL, WHY AREN'T *YOU* THERE WITH EVERYBODY ELSE?

M—MAYBE I FORGOT SOMETHING...

OH, REALLY? WHAT?

WHAT'S IT TO YOU IF I DID? *NOBODY* EVER CARES WHAT I DO.

THIS!

HEY, *WAIT!*

WHAT WAS THAT SHE GRABBED OFF THE SHELF?

LOOKED LIKE A BIG JAR OF *CHEMICALS.*

THERE SHE GOES, INTO THE *STAIRWELL!*

THE WAY SHE'S HANGING ONTO THAT JAR, THOUGH, TELLS ME WHATEVER'S INSIDE IS *KEY* TO THE MYSTERY I'M TRYING TO SOLVE.

YEAH, *ABOUT* THAT "MYSTERY," FRANK--

--YOU *DO* REALIZE YOU AND JOE NEVER TOLD CHET AND ME WHAT THE BIG "MYSTERY" IS ABOUT THESE ZOMBIE CRAWLS YOU'RE INVESTIGATING?

OH. AH.

HM.

A FRIEND OF A FRIEND GOT *HURT* AT ONE, AND WE'RE JUST WORRIED SOMETHING'S NOT RIGHT.

SOMETHING'S "NOT RIGHT," ALL RIGHT--AND IT'S THAT *STORY* YOU JUST TOLD ME.

WHY DON'T YOU JUST TELL ME WHAT'S *REALLY* GOING ON?

BECAUSE JOE AND I PROMISED DAD WE'D NEVER TELL *ANYONE* WE'RE SECRETLY WORKING FOR A.T.A.C.

TIMES LIKE THIS, HAVING TO MIS-LEAD A FRIEND, I ALMOST *REGRET* THAT PROMISE.

BAYPORT HIGH.

STAY AWAY FROM ME, FRANK HARDY!

ONE MORE STEP AND YOU'LL **NEVER** FIND OUT WHAT MADE THE KIDS AT THOSE **ZOMBIE CRAWLS** ACT LIKE THEY WERE **BRAIN DEAD.**

I'M **GUESSING** IT'S GOT SOMETHING TO DO WITH WHAT'S IN THAT **CONTAINER,** TAYLOR.

WHAT I **DON'T** UNDERSTAND IS **WHY** YOU'D WANT TO **HURT** ANYONE.

YOU **KIDDING** ME?

THE WAY PEOPLE TREAT "GEEKS" LIKE ME, WHY **WOULDN'T** I WANT TO HURT SOMEONE?

CHAPTER FIVE: ZOMBIES ON PARADE

WHEN I MOVED TO BAYPORT FROM *RIVER HEIGHTS*, I THOUGHT I'D HAVE A CHANCE TO START OVER, MAKE *FRIENDS*, GET A LIFE.

INSTEAD, IT WAS THE SAME HERE AS IT'S BEEN *EVERYWHERE ELSE*.

YOU ALL *IGNORED* ME!

YOUR *GIRLFRIEND* DOESN'T EVEN KNOW I'VE BEEN IN THE SAME *SCIENCE CLASS* WITH HER FOR *TWO YEARS!*

ACTUALLY, BELINDA ISN'T TECHNICALLY MY "GIRLFRIEND"...

NOBODY *CARES* WHETHER I'M DEAD OR ALIVE!

YOU TREAT ME LIKE SOME KIND OF *MINDLESS ZOMBIE*.

TAYLOR, CALM DOWN. JUST TELL US WHAT YOU'VE DONE.

SO I FIGURED, TURNABOUT IS *FAIR PLAY*.

I CAME UP WITH A DRUG THAT WIPES OUT *WILL POWER*.

THEN I FOUND SOMEONE WHO PAID ME TO *USE* IT.

SOMEBODY PAID YOU? *WHO?*

I'M **SCARED**, FRANK!

JOE **ISN'T ANSWERING** HIS CELL PHONE-- NEITHER IS CHET!

WHAT IF WE'RE ALREADY **TOO LATE**--?

LOOK, BELINDA, I KNOW MY LITTLE BROTHER CAN COME OFF PRETTY **HEADSTRONG** NOW AND THEN--

SCREEE

--BUT NO MATTER HOW **DEEP** A HOLE HE DIGS FOR HIMSELF, SOMEHOW HE ALWAYS MANAGES TO CLIMB OUT IN ONE PIECE.

TRUST ME. JOE MAY END UP COVERED IN MUD, BUT HE'LL BE **FINE**.

HEAR THAT, JOE?

I'M COUNTING ON YOU NOT TO GET YOURSELF **KILLED**...

C'MON, C'MON--KEEP MOVIN'! UP THE STEPS! WE HAVEN'T GOT ALL NIGHT!

HEY, MILT, WATCH FOR STRAGGLERS! DON'T LET ANY OF THESE IDIOTS WANDER OFF BEFORE THE JOB'S DONE!

GOTCHA, RICKY!

W-WARNING YOU KIDS--

IF-IF YOU DON'T BACK OFF--

HNNNNUUHHHHHHNN-NNUUHHHHUUH

I-I'LL S-SHOOT!

GGGGNNRRGGHH!

MONSTER!

ATTACKING US...

...H-HAVE TO STOP HIM!

CHAPTER SIX: THE MONSTER INSIDE ME

T-THIS IS WRONG... ALL WRONG...

MY HEAD... FEELS LIKE...IT'S ON FIRE...

... HAVE TO... PUT THE FIRE OUT...

UH, CROOKS? STATUE?

YOU MEAN THOSE *THREE THUGS* CHET AND I SPOTTED--THEY'RE HERE TO ROB THE *MUSEUM!*

USING THIS OUT-OF-CONTROL *ZOMBIE CRAWL* TO COVER THEIR *GETAWAY.*

"AS LONG AS THESE 'ZOMBIES' ARE UNDER THE INFLUENCE OF TAYLOR DENT'S TRICK MAKEUP, THEY'LL BLOCK THE POLICE FROM GETTING IN..."

"... WHILE THE CROOKS HAVE A CLEAR PATH *OUT.*"

SO WHY ARE YOU RE-WIRING THE *FIRE ALARM?*

I'M NOT JUST *RE-WIRING* THE ALARM, JOE...

BREEBREEBREEEEBREE

--I'M *SETTING IT OFF*--

--BECAUSE WHEN THE *FIRE ALARM* GOES OFF--

NNUHHNN UHHNHH

--SO DO THE *FIRE SPRINKLERS!*

uhhuhuh uhhuh hhh

I GET IT! WHEN I *SOAKED* MYSELF, I WASHED THE MAKEUP OFF--

--AND THAT BROKE THE *ZOMBIE MIND-CONTROL.*

I FIGURED THE EASIEST WAY TO *REVERSE* A GROUP BRAIN-WASHING--

"--WAS A *GROUP RINSE!*"

UH NUNHH UHHH

...UH?

Uuhuhhhhh

AH, WOULD SOMEBODY PLEASE EXPLAIN WHAT HAPPENED TO ME, AND WHY I'M ALL WET?

I'LL INFORM A.T.A.C. WHAT YOU'VE DISCOVERED. THEY'LL DECIDE HOW TO PROCEED.

GOOD WORK, BOTH OF YOU.

THANKS, DAD.

FRANK, I KNOW YOU AND JOE HAD *DIFFERENT POINTS OF VIEW* ABOUT HOW TO APPROACH THIS MISSION--

I GUESS THAT'S *ONE* WAY TO LOOK AT IT.

HOW WOULD *YOU* LOOK AT IT, BIG BROTHER?

YOU WENT OFF HALF-COCKED, *WITHOUT* A PLAN, AND ALMOST GOT YOURSELF AND CHET *KILLED.*

BUT WE *WEREN'T* KILLED, AND IF I HADN'T BEEN THERE, AND JUMPED IN THAT *FOUNTAIN,* YOU WOULDN'T HAVE FIGURED OUT HOW TO *STOP* THE CROOKS' GETAWAY.

YOU TOOK A *DUMB RISK,* JOE.

IT WAS A *CALCULATED* RISK, AND I'D DO IT AGAIN

NOT IF I HAVE ANYTHING TO SAY ABOUT IT.

YOU **WON'T.** YOU'RE MY **BROTHER,** NOT MY BOSS.

WHAT YOU ARE, IS A **TEAM.** BROTHERS **AND** PARTNERS.

YOU'RE ALSO **BOTH** ABOUT TO BE LATE FOR **SCHOOL.**

DAD'S RIGHT. WE CAN TALK ABOUT THIS **LATER.**

HI, MOM.

BYE, MOM.

FRANK, JOE...

DID I HEAR THE BOYS **ARGUING** ABOUT SOMETHING? IS ANYTHING **WRONG?**

OUR SONS HAVE BEEN "THE HARDY BOYS" SO LONG SOMETIMES WE FORGET THEY'RE **TWO DIFFERENT YOUNG MEN,** WITH THEIR OWN MINDS, AND THEIR OWN **POINTS OF VIEW.**

SHOULD WE BE **WORRIED** ABOUT THEM, FENTON?

LAURA, I WISH I KNEW.

BUT I HAVE A FEELING OUR BOYS ARE FACING SOME **TOUGH** TIMES.

I JUST **HOPE** THEY CONTINUE TO FACE THEM **TOGETHER.**

NEXT: "BREAK-UP!"

WATCH OUT FOR PAPERCUT**Z**

Welcome to the premiere edition of the all-new THE HARDY BOYS The New Case Files graphic novel series! I'm Jim Salicrup, Editor-in-Chief of Papercutz, publisher of graphic novels for all-ages. If you were a follower of The Hardy Boy's first graphic novel series, welcome back! If you're new to The Hardy Boys in comics form, well, you're in for a wild ride! THE HARDY BOYS is just as action-packed and exciting in comics form as they are in their prose series.

In fact, we strive to preserve all the things that have made The Hardy Boys so popular and successful in their book series in our all-new graphic novel stories. To that end we've enlisted Gerry Conway to write THE HARDY BOYS The New Case Files. Gerry is a legendary comics writer, responsible for some of the most unforgettable comics ever published. Taking over *The Amazing Spider-Man* comic after co-creator Stan Lee left the series, Gerry shocked a generation of Spidey-fans when he killed-off Peter Parker's then true love, Gwen Stacy. Gerry quickly followed that up with Spidey's brutal battle with the Green Goblin. Even if you didn't read the comics, you probably saw it brought to dramatic life on the big screen in the very first blockbuster *Spider-Man* movie. If that wasn't enough, Gerry also created The Punisher, who has also inspired several movie adaptations as well. I could go on and on about Gerry's countless comicbook accomplishments, but then we wouldn't have enough room for any comics in this graphic novel. I will mention though, that back when I was editing the *Spider-Man* titles for Marvel, it was a dream come true to work with Mr. Conway. He understands what makes for exciting, emotionally powerful comics better than anyone—so you can imagine how thrilled we are at Papercutz to have Gerry writing the new adventures of Frank and Joe Hardy. And just as he forever shook up the very foundations of poor Peter Parker's world—expect Gerry to do the same with The Hardy Boys starting right now! Whatever you do, don't miss THE HARDY BOYS The New Case Files #2—the title truly says it all: "Break-Up!"

And speaking of titles, you won't want to miss the premiere of NANCY DREW The New Case Files #1 "Vampire Slayer" Part One. If you're the macho type who thinks that Nancy's graphic novel exploits may be "too girly" for you, you have to see what happens when Nancy meets Gregor Coffin! Is he man or vampire?! We guarantee you never saw a Nancy Drew story like this one before! And if that wasn't enough of a reason, let me mention what sharp-eyed Hardy Boys fans probably already discovered a few pages back—that Taylor Dent is from Nancy Drew's hometown of River Heights. Something strange sure is going on around here—or should I say, over there! Just to give you a little taste of what we're talking about regarding America's favorite Girl Detective we're offering a special preview of NANCY DREW The New Case Files #1 "Vampire Slayer" on the pages following! Check out this small sample, written by Stefan Petrucha and Sarah Kinney, and drawn by Sho Murase, and see if you can resist picking up your own copies of the complete 2-part epic!

That's it for now, but please take a moment to tell us what YOU think of THE HARDY BOYS The New Case Files #1. Either email me at salicrup@papercutz.com or send a letter to The Hardy Boys, c/o PAPERCUTZ, 40 Exchange Place, Suite 1308, New York, NY 10005. We hope to present some of the most interesting comments in our very next volume! Till then, watch out for Papercutz!

Thanks,

Jim

Special preview of NANCY DREW
The New Case Files #1 "Vampire Slayer" Part One!

THAT'S ME, *NANCY DREW, GIRL DETECTIVE,* THE ONE WITH THE CROSSBOW AND THE ATTITUDE.

I DON'T KNOW *HOW* I LET YOU TWO TALK ME INTO THIS!

COME ON, NANCE! IF WE SHOW UP TO THE MOVIE IN COSTUME WE GET IN FOR HALF PRICE!

AND GEORGE AND I HAVE ALREADY SEEN IT *FOUR* TIMES, SO WE *NEED* TO SAVE SOME MONEY!

THE OTHER TWO ARE MY FRIENDS, GEORGE AND BESS.

USUALLY I'M DRAGGING THEM SOMEPLACE DANGEROUS, SO I FIGURE IT'S ONLY FAIR TO LET THEM DRAG ME OUT ONCE IN A WHILE.

HEY, AT LEAST *YOU* DON'T HAVE FAKE *WEREWOLF* HAIR PLASTERED OVER YOUR FACE!

NOW, NOW! YOU MAKE A *LOVELY* WOLF!

THEN AGAIN, THE SHORTCUT THROUGH THE CEMETERY I SUGGESTED TURNED OUT TO BE MORE DANGEROUS THAN I THOUGHT.

DID YOU GUYS *HEAR* SOME- THING?

AS A DARK FIGURE LEAPT OVER THE GRAVESTONE I WAS THINKING THIS PROBABLY WOULD HAVE BEEN *MUCH* MORE FRIGHTENING IF I ACTUALLY BELIEVED IN VAMPIRES.

THEN I REALIZED, IT WAS PRETTY MUCH AS FRIGHTENING AS IT COULD GET NO MATTER *WHAT* I BELIEVED.

NANCY DREW
VAMPIRE SLAYER Part One

NANCY!

WHAT'S THE PLAN?

RUN!

IT WASN'T ALWAYS MY BEST *PLAN*, BUT IT DID WORK SOMETIMES.

UNLESS WHOEVER WAS CHASING YOU TURNS OUT TO BE MUCH *FASTER*.

I'M GENERALLY *NOT* THE VIOLENT TYPE, BUT IT DIDN'T FEEL LIKE I HAD MUCH CHOICE HERE.

OF COURSE THE CROSSBOW WAS *FAKE*, PART OF MY SLAYER COSTUME.

BUT TALL DARK AND *FANGY* HERE DIDN'T KNOW THAT.

AND THAT TRICK *WORKED.*

MOSTLY, I WAS THINKING, "*PHEW!*"

BUT I WAS ALSO THINKING I'D AT LEAST HAVE A SECOND TO FIGURE OUT WHAT WAS GOING ON.

UNFORTUNATELY, THE FIRST THING I FIGURED OUT WAS THAT THE "VAMPIRE" PROBABLY WASN'T CHASING US AT *ALL.*

HE WAS *BEING* CHASED...

...BY MY DOG.

TOGO!

TOGO LIKES TO COME ALONG WHEN I GO OUT SOMETIMES, AND I GUESS I FORGOT TO LATCH HIS DOGGIE-DOOR!

HEY, IF HE *WASN'T* A REAL VAMPIRE, WHY ISN'T HE HERE ON LINE WITH THE REST OF US?

MAYBE HE'S ALREADY *INSIDE?*

ONCE WE WERE WATCHING THE MOVIE, I WAS *AMAZED.* NOT BY THE FILM, BUT BY HOW BESS AND GEORGE COULD SEE SOMETHING SO *MANY* TIMES AND STILL BE TOTALLY *GRIPPED!*

IT'S SO *ROMANTIC!*

AND TERRIFYING!

I KIND OF GOT OVER THE WHOLE VAMPIRE THING AFTER I READ *DRACULA* IN THE FIFTH GRADE.

I DON'T KNOW, THE WHOLE BLOOD-SUCKING THING JUST DIDN'T APPEAL.

CRIMES ASIDE, ONE OF THE BIGGEST MYSTERIES I'VE EVER TRIED TO SOLVE IS WHY PEOPLE LIKE WHAT THEY LIKE.

STILL WORKING ON THAT ONE.

I DID NOTICE THAT THE GUY FROM THE GRAVEYARD *WASN'T* HERE. MAYBE HE WAS GOING TO A *LATER* SHOW?

I ALSO NOTICED SOMETHING ELSE.

Get the complete story in NANCY DREW The New Case Files #1 "Vampire Slayer" Part One - Available at booksellers everywhere!